R Reality

R Reality

Mackenzie Truss

Contact
Information:
https://mackenzietruss.wixsite.com/my-site

Front cover designed by: Dolcevitadesign
Editor: Andrea Leeth

ISBN: 9798864936702

For my family, whom I cherish dearly.

Prologue

As I look at the lab work in front of me, I feel that my research will never come to an end. My life is hectic, consisting of test tubes, new antidotes, sleepless nights in the lab, and lots of energy drinks. My name is Jacob Sims, and I am twenty-two years old. I volunteer at one of Georgia's largest research institutions. My team members and I theorized that there is a pre-birth world that everyone has been to before they were born. According to data collected through personal stories in this world, souls fight each other for the chance to be born. The rules are simple: if you win the fight, then you will be born; if you don't, you stay in the pre-birth world until you overpower a rival soul. We believe that your soul has already seen a preview of the life it could have if it were to win the fight. For instance, you already look as if you were a full-grown human being.

I got stopped on the street all the time by angry pedestrians who heard our theories about this world. They often became offended and yelled, "What gives you and your group the right to say this is where we come from? How do you know? You can't remember!" Sorry to break it to you, but the thing is, we did remember.

It all started fourteen years ago, when a small percentage of people had this recurring vision of themselves in a foreign place, covered in blood, fighting to the death with someone they had no recollection of meeting, then later being born as a baby. Soon, people all over the world had these same visions. After a few months, the group theorized it could be a "pre-birth world," and the first step to human life. There was only one problem though, the rest of the human population couldn't remember such a world and it wouldn't be easy convincing them. The group took it among themselves to show society the truth. They named themselves "R.B.," which stands for "Remember Before." For the past few years, R.B. has been creating antidotes (or trials, as we refer to them) that will make our society remember the pre-birth world.

Every month, we come out with a new trial. We test each new trial on someone who cannot remember their former life. Someone who supports the cause yet is relatively unimportant to the overall production of the mission. Someone mental enough to sign a potential death wish for a greater cause, and there is only one person who is willing to do this job: me.

We completed fifteen trials. Each trial received a letter from the alphabet. Trials A through Q were all unsuccessful. Thankfully, these failed trials have not been fatal, as they only send me into a deep sleep. When testing trials A through Q, I saw inside the pre-birth world although I couldn't explore it. In a few days, trial R will be ready for me to test.

We get the antidote by collecting the hormone released through a team members' sweat or saliva as they have a flashback of the pre-birth world. The hormone is then injected into my body so I can enter the pre-birth world. The other trials failed because we didn't know how much of the hormone we needed. A fear among the group is that too much of the hormone could kill the tester. The members of R.B. strongly encourage each other to be careful with the dosage because I am the only tester they have and probably the only one they ever will.

One morning, three members of R.B. and I walked down a side street to arrive at the lab. It was late January, and we were bundled up in unreasonable layers of scarves and coats. The streets were quiet, as if the snow-covered ground had buried the city's people. All of a sudden, we were attacked by a group of teenagers behind us. They jumped and beat us to the ground. They screamed that we were wasting our time. That we were cowards. That we were despicable and going to hell because our theory rebelled against religious beliefs. As they walked off, the blonde-haired boy turned his head back and looked me up and down as if I were a wild animal, yet there was a sense of longing in his eyes. Luke was the boy's name and he used to be my best friend, years ago. He was the equivalent of a brother to me until we reached the age of fifteen. At the time, R.B. was just developing their theories and ideas about the pre-birth world. They shared their theory with the society, and after a while, the society recoiled. Since then, there has been an unspoken rule to not show interest in R.B.'s theories in the hopes that the organization would be forgotten.

Naturally, I didn't hear about this "unspoken rule" and didn't deny my fascination with the beliefs of R.B. It seems a lifetime ago that I was talking to Luke about R.B. and I didn't understand why he was uncomfortable about the topic. I stopped talking about it and changed the subject and his uneasiness seemed to waver. Until the next day when he mentioned it over the dinner table, in front of my parents. After many months, numerous people found out that

I was a supporter of R.B. and that I was a potential danger to society. The more people found out, the more my parents became ashamed of me. I wanted to have a purpose in my life and not have to hide because of my parents' embarrassment anymore, so I did what was best for me. I left and joined R.B.

Some members of R.B. were not fond of me at first because I was an outsider and young, to say the least. When I came, I didn't think this was much better than living in the society because I still felt like an outsider. However, when I slid under the sheets of my bed and waited for sleep to take hold of me, I realized that I had a purpose here and I was finally needed, even if I wasn't necessarily appreciated. I never fathomed that a group of strangers would feel more supportive of my beliefs than my family would.

Chapter 1

"Jacob." A familiar voice called through my dreams. "Come on man, we are ready," Ian said as he shook my shoulders. My eyes fluttered open, and a tall, skinny man in a white lab coat looked down at me in my small cot. He nudged my shoulder, his dark curly hair creeped into his eyes. With a fatigued sigh, he scoffed. "Jacob, I'm serious! Get up, you were late for the last test. You can't be late again!"

I stretched and said in a gruff voice, "Are they still mad about that?" "Well, I would be too if I stayed up all night working on an antidote and you were late to test it. It makes you look like you don't care," he said, irritated. "I don't think you fully understand how hard we work sometimes." I opened my mouth to object, but he cut me off. "Go get dressed."

I walked across the cold gray floor, careful not to crinkle the research papers I failed to pick up last night. I maneuvered to the bathroom sink and splash my face with water. As I looked in the mirror, a young man with dark-green eyes and brown messy hair stared back at me. I could only conjure up two words to describe the figure that starred back at me: pure exhaustion. I could not pinpoint if it was exhaustion from his endless work hours or losing hope of filling a void in his life. A void that told him something is incomplete.

Ian and I depart from our sleep units and navigate down the long hallway. The corridor is dim and cold, adding to that void I feel deep inside. I brushed off the thought and kept walking. Heavy metal doors await us as we step inside the testing room. It's bare, with only a small cot, a monitor, and an IV bag hooked onto a stand. Our building is small and rundown, consisting of broken sinks and fixtures in need of repair. Since R.B. isn't on good terms with our society, we had to make do with any space we could. Some would look at our facility and say that we are underfunded. When in reality, we are not funded at all. The members of R.B. and I have each poured our life savings into this project. But it's worth it to fight for what we believe in. To prove that the pre-birth world exists and is the first stage of life.

"We are ready for you," said a short, middle-aged man in a white lab coat. His coat was wrinkled and stained. The hand stitched name of "Paul," embroidered on the front, frayed in every which way, proved its years of use. He stirred the antidote in a small glass container. Paul, the man who founded R.B. and our lead scientist, looked up at me through his wire-framed glasses. "Take a seat," he said, motioning toward the cot with his gloved hands.

As I lay down, he went over the protocol. "Lay still while the hormone enters your body. To enter the pre-birth world, you will allow the hormone to spread, this will put you into a sleep as your body adjusts to the hormone. Once your body is adjusted, you will enter the pre-birth world." As Paul began to give the directions, I began to compile all of the information I had gathered thus far about this foreign world.

I will then see a plethora of people in a vast darkness fighting each other. Blue orbs of lights will also begin to float around the group of people.

"To leave the pre-birth world you have to find a way to mentally dissociate from what you are seeing."

One trick I learned to dissociate from the pre-birth world was to imagine I was closing a door.

"Brain waves are not shown on the monitor while you are in the pre-birth world. When you disconnect yourself, brain waves will appear on the monitor and that's how we know we need to stop the hormone and take out the IV. You will wake up shortly after."

He walked swiftly to the table, and after a few minutes of preparation, he sat on the edge of the cot, flicked the needle, and stuck it into my arm. This was the part I hated most. The hormone stung as it entered my bloodstream, not to mention Ian snickered the entire time and later called me immature as he knew needles made me squeamish. I didn't have to put up with him for too long because after a few minutes, I began to see black spots in my vision. The black spots turned into black masses, and eventually all I saw was darkness.

Seconds later, I arrived in the pre-birth world. The temperature turned cold and made the hair on my arms stand up. No sound could be heard, only the beat of my heart and the rhythm of my breathing. Blue orbs appeared as ghostly blue light radiated around them. I had recorded this in a previous trial and our theory was that these blue orbs of light were newly formed souls that hadn't seen a preview of what they'd look like in their future life. Hundreds of human figures emerged from the darkness. By an unknown force, I was taken to a scene where I was fighting an opponent and the hundreds of people in the black abyss disappeared.

I finally saw *myself*, which is a first for our team. The previous trials we tested were unable to show this evidence due to the little amount of the hormone in my system. Trial R worked. I didn't exclaim over this finding. I was only here to lay eyes on my soul. When I was about to mentally disconnect from the pre-birth world, a warm voice popped inside my head.

"It's me. I'm still here." The voice was familiar, similar to my own, though I second-guessed if it came from my internal dialog. But this voice was not mine. I looked around, making sure no one was near.

"No, look in front of you. It's me, I'm here."

I had an eerie feeling the person in front of me was not *my* soul.

"Help me," he said.

What the hell? I took deep breaths. *Calm down, you're over thinking. No one's inside your head, no one is here that can talk. You've never made it this far inside the pre-birth world and you are getting nervous. Calm down. Disconnect.*

"No, you can't leave me yet, Jacob!" the voice urged. "You have to get me out of this place. You're the only one who can help me." His gruff, yet innocent voice rang in my ears and bounced around in my head.

"Who are you?" I spat out, more like a whisper, as my heart felt like it would beat out of my chest.

"I'm your unborn twin."

Chapter 2

"W-what?"

"I was supposed to be born with you, but you won your fight and I lost mine. This is *my* soul you are looking at, not yours." There was a long moment of silence as I stared blankly at him, unsure what to do, what to say. For the first time since I left my family, I felt frightened and concerned. No one had ever spoken in the pre-birth world. Should I trust his heavy claim? Was I hallucinating or had the effects of this experiment caught up with me? *What if the hormone injection messed with my brain chemistry? He can't be real.*

"Just tell me what to do. You're better at this than I am. I need to be born!"

Taken aback by his introduction, I stammered out, "No, I ca—"

"Jacob! Help me!"

"I-I, I have to go."

"No, please! I can't fight anymore."

"I only have a certain amount of time here. They need me back," I said, out of breath.

He sighed. "You'll help me later, right, Jacob?"

"No, this is insane. I'm probably going insane."

"Don't leave me here! Please!"

"How do I know you're real? Why should I believe that you are my twin?" I stared at him for an answer; he had no response.

"I have no way to prove this to you. All I know is that I feel a strong connection toward you."

"You're not real." I pressed.

I can also talk to you in your mind, he said inside my head.

"Stop doing that!"

"Do you believe me now? It's me! Your twin," he said innocently.

"I guess, I believe you. I should get going now."

"You promise you'll come back?" he begged again.

"Yes, I will... How have you never won a fight but you've been in the pre-birth world for twenty-two years?"

"Don't pretend like this is a piece of cake. I watched you struggle and you barely made it out." I looked at his *body*, covered in a plethora of bruises and cuts. Open wounds trickled a steady stream of blood, black-and-blue bruises marked his throat, and bones poked out. I came to a heart-wrenching realization. He was dying, even though he hadn't been born yet. I was about to say something until he cut me off. "With every fight a soul loses, they grow ten times weaker for their next fight. The odds of the soul winning the second fight are slim to none. I assume it's a way to see who is strong enough to handle life. It's survival of the fittest." I let this sink in, my mind wandering off.

"What's your name?"

"I don't have one … yet." I pondered this and felt a stab of sadness within me. He truly did look just like me. I knew to anyone else my "twin" revelation would sound absurd. However, considering this is the pre-birth world, the rules of absurdity were different. We stood in a foreign dimension, if you would call it, and the chance of me having an unborn twin seemed to be the most realistic dynamic of R.B.'s discovery.

"Ethan. My parents debated naming me that anyway."

"Ethan, my name's Ethan." I could almost hear the smile in his voice and it warmed my heart.

"I do have to go now, it's getting late," I said with reluctance.

"You'll come back, right?"

"Every day until I get you out. I'll help you win." I disconnected and felt myself rise back into my reality.

—

"So, what did you get?" Paul blurted out. I opened my eyes. I hated when he did this because I needed to get my bearings straight before a bombardment of questions. I shot him an irritated look and sat up. *What did I find?* I found my unborn twin but if I said this, they might exploit him. Ethan was my business and mine alone; the pre-birth world was *their* business. I couldn't tell them that I already saw "myself" fight because I never did. I only saw Ethan, so technically, *my* soul was still floating around somewhere in the vast darkness getting pummeled. "Jacob, did you see yourself?"

"No ... I didn't."

"Okay," he said with an exasperated sigh. "We will try again tomorrow. Until then do as usual and record any new findings."

—

When I fell asleep that night, I had a dream, more of a flashback, when I was an infant. My mother held me in her arms while she and my father smiled and looked down at their wonderful new baby. My father said something that made my mother laugh and I looked at the baby-blue balloon tied to the banister. My eyes wandered up the string, focused on the color of the balloon, then fixated on the corner of the ceiling. At first, I saw nothing, but the longer I stared, an almost transparent

21

face of a man with green eyes and short brown hair stared back at me. My infant eyes didn't know who it was then, but now I knew. It was Ethan. He had watched his twin live a life meant for two my entire existence. His face was as white as a piece of paper as if a wave of nausea hit him. He missed out on this life, feeling hopeless and forgotten.

"What's he staring at up there?" My mother laughed. My eyes snapped over to her, but when I glanced back to the corner, Ethan was gone.

—

I had been awake since four a.m. and attempted to come up with ways that I could help Ethan win. I've brainstormed things I could tell Paul that would buy me more time in the pre-birth world. I couldn't keep telling them that I haven't found anything. Six a.m. rolls around and there was no knock on my door from Ian. Everything is quiet.

Maybe they're just running behind. As I step out of my room, the hallway is still dark. I flipped on the light switch and saw that the laboratory doors were closed and the lights were off too.

R.B. never takes days off, ever. I shrugged it off and pulled the lab doors open, turned the machines on, got the hormone ready, and injected myself with it. I hoped that no one walked in. I was told since the first day that I began volunteering as a tester that under no circumstances was I allowed to enter the pre-birth world without the team waiting on the other side to retrieve me. Without much thought, I cast this rule aside. Ethan is more important, and he was currently the only *person* who seemed to care about me. Within minutes, the blue orbs of light engulfed my vision, and I was taken to what I hoped is my soul but there was a chance it could be Ethan's.

"Ethan, I'm here," I said in my head. All of a sudden, the opponent *my* soul was fighting wrapped his large hands around my throat. I watched as I gasped for air and slowly turned blue right before I fell to the ground. I had an inkling that this was not my soul before me and decided to reach out to my brother again.

"Ethan?" Still no response. "Ethan!" I yelled. Seconds later, he gasped inside my head. "Ethan! Are you okay? What the hell just happened?"

He responded with a gasp and a loud cough. "I-I died again. I need you to start doing something! Help me win!" he exclaimed in my head.

"That's what I was going—"

"Not again! Please, I need a break!" Ethan screamed, his plea echoing, and he disappeared into the dark abyss.

Chapter 3

"Ethan …" I called into the darkness before his lifeless *body* rose onto its feet, but this time, his body was paler and he looked *sicker.* This time, he was fighting a redheaded girl who looked … she looked perfectly healthy. She must have been a new, unharmed soul.

"Okay, tell me what to do Jacob," he said as I hesitated.

"Punch her."

"But … she's a girl."

"So?"

"It's—"

Get a grip, Ethan.

"Punch her," I spat out.

"Where?" He had waited too late. She'd already kicked him in the groin, and while he was hunched over in pain, she drove her elbows into the nape of his neck. Which made him fall to his knees.

Gosh, he is terrible at this.

"I can hear you, Jacob!"

"Get up and punch her!" He rose and punched her hard in the nose, making her stumble backward as blood trickled from her nose. He punched her over and over, grabbed her head and bashed it hard on the cement floor. It's almost as if he had unleashed twenty-two years' worth of anger.

"There you go! Keep going!" I encouraged him. She picked herself off the ground; his beatings barely fazed her. He is too weak; *how will he ever win?* He mustered up enough power to knock her out. As she lay on the floor, Ethan continued to throw his petty punches as she stayed perfectly still. "Ethan." He threw another punch. "Ethan." He raised his fist again, ignoring me. "Ethan!"

"What?"

"She's gone, save your strength."

"I won? I won!" he said breathlessly. His voice was no longer in my head; it was coming from his body. He looked at me with his back to the girl. When I began to process that he killed her, the redheaded girl stumbled up, ran behind him as fast as lightning, bared her teeth, and bit a gruesome piece of flesh out of his neck, severing his artery. Blood gushed from his skinned neck and splattered the center of my shirt. Ethan's body slowly fell to the ground, then dissipated. He had lost yet another match. I waited for him to come back. *If that was Ethan's body, where am I? Where is my body?*

"I see *your* body all the time. For instance, you're right over there," he coughed as he pointed behind him to the left.

"There is nothing over there but a boy fighting the open air."

"No, he's fighting you," he said with a laugh. I almost felt like I might go crazy until I told myself, *he just died, don't believe anything he says. He's probably not in his right mind.* I agreed with him, only because I needed to get going. I had spent too much time here as it was. I wondered what would happen to Ethan when I left?

"Do you fight all day?"

"No, we never have more than two fights a day, some days we only have one fight. They happen spontaneously."

"Then what do you do when you're done fighting for the day?"

"We just float around." He motioned to the darkness around us. "We torment the new souls, you know, the blue orbs?" He chuckled.

"I know what they are. I'm a researcher, we are studying this place," I responded in a daze as he concentrated hard for a moment before he asked, "What is a researcher?"

I didn't have time to give him a vocabulary lesson today. "I have to go now."

"Go? But you just got here." He continued to talk, but I ignored him as my thoughts spiraled.

How will I get back? When I disconnect, there will be no one to pull me out of the pre-birth world. No one knows I'm here.

Suddenly, I felt as if I had snorted water up my nose. My throat burned and I panicked just before the sensation vanished. I opened my eyes and saw Paul's furious eyes staring down at me. I gasped for air and wrapped my hands around my burning throat. "Hurts, doesn't it?" Paul yelled.

"What did you do to me?" I croaked.

"We had to pull your IV out because we couldn't get you to disconnect." I looked at my arm, a dot of blood exposed from where the IV was removed. I wiped the blood off with my finger and then on my blood-stained shirt.

"What were you thinking going in there alone? Anything could have happened Jacob!"

"What the hell is on his shirt?" Ian squinted. "Is that blood?"

"Whose blood is that?" Paul's assistant, Michael, asked.

"I-I don't know," I stuttered.

"Jacob, are you hiding something? What are you not telling us? Why were you in there for so long?" Paul pressed with a deep crease between his brows.

"Nothing, I'm not hiding anything."

"If you know something we don't, you better tell us right now. I'm tired of these absurd reports from you. I need answers! You are wasting our time and the little money we have."

I hesitated and told the truth. "I can't find myself in there. I can only see other people."

"Then why were you in there for so long Jacob? Why is your shirt covered in blood?" he said as his face turned red with every breath. I glanced at Ian for some help.

"Paul, if he says he doesn't know, he doesn't know." Ian looked down at me from where I sat in the chair and took note of my shirt. "Let's just take the shirt for analysis, it could be useful information."

"Fine, take it." Paul scoffed as he turned to me. "I am serious Jacob, find out how to get this experiment going. I'm tired of sitting around wasting my time because you can't give us any information. If you can't give me what I need, I'll find someone who can. You're not that irreplaceable."

—

Later in the night, Ian walked into the kitchen, perplexed. I sat at the table as he stood in front of me.

"I thought you said you didn't know whose blood this was, Jacob."

"I don't," I lied.

"What? How could you not know?"

"What do you mean 'how could I not know?' I didn't see—"

"It's all your blood, Jacob! So, you did see your body in there." His eyes widened with a look of excitement. "I'm confused though ... you said you weren't able to see anything in there ... Nothing you're saying is adding up." I stared blankly at him, not sure what to say next as he blurted out, "What the hell happened in there?"

It was Ethan's blood, not mine. I thought to myself.

"Jacob!" Paul interrupted, ducking his head in the doorway. I looked up at him. "Quit wasting time and go get to work," he snapped. Ian and I exchanged glances.

"Now!"

"Okay, okay. I'm going."

Before I walked out the doorway, Ian said suspiciously from behind me, "Be careful Jacob. This entire project lies in your hands. Don't screw it up."

Chapter 4

I sat at my desk with the light from my old laptop casting shadows on the walls. *Our* world is currently equipped with the most sophisticated and groundbreaking technology since computers came out nearly five hundred years ago. Since R.B. had to buy all their own equipment, they were only able to afford computers. I wonder how much easier my research would be if I had access to the technology available in our society. As I typed away on the keyboard, my train of thought was broken.

"I'm your unborn twin." His voice chimed inside my memory. I'd heard of the word "twin" but didn't know much about it. I typed "twins" into the search bar on my laptop. All the links revealed an "Access denied" page, except for two on the last page of the results. The first successful link led me to a page that described a woman who had written about a dream where she had an identical twin sister in the year 2040. She had seen an alternate reality where her twin sister and her went through life together and were best friends. When she woke up, she described a deep void within her and a longing to get her other half back. She wrote a book describing the dream and she was applauded for the emotional impact she had on her

readers. When I read her story, I couldn't help but relate to this unfamiliar woman as we shared the same bond toward our siblings. She brought me comfort, as I had never felt that I could relate to someone in this way. I took the opportunity to print her article, which also had her picture. I folded the paper in my pocket to keep with me to feel encouraged.

The second working link led me to an article titled, "The History of Twins." The first line stated: "Hundreds of years ago, it was said that identical twins have the same DNA. Twins have been extinct for hundreds of years. There has been no known record of a pair of twins since the late 2,000s."

Then why were Ethan and I meant to be twins? Is something holding him back?

Identical twins wouldn't have become extinct for no reason. It's a genetic mutation. What if something has been keeping twins from being born for more than five hundred years? Why can't I see myself in the pre-birth world, but Ethan can see me? Why is it that when I enter the pre-birth world, I see him first?

What if it all has something to do with DNA? Since we are identical twins and share the same DNA, maybe that's why I can see him. But the question is, how do I see myself?

A static-filled, muffled voice whispers inside my head. *"They have to mix."* The light blue glow that came from my computer screen gave the now pitch-black room an eerie feeling. The hairs on my arms stood straight as Ethan's voice echoed from the pre-birth world, wherever that may be.

Mix what? DNA?

"Mix … the DNA … of your soul … with the … DNA of… your body," he whispered as it sent chills through my body. His DNA is identical to mine and now all I had to do was combine my blood with the blood-stained shirt from this morning. That was until I realized that I already had … I wiped the blood from the IV on my shirt. Maybe this is why I heard him even in the real world, because a connection was already made. Maybe this meant that I would finally see myself when I go back tomorrow.

There was a small beep from my computer and the screen went black.

Chapter 5

As the dreadful sound of my alarm clock flooded the barely sunlit room, I immediately felt hollow inside. I trudged into the bathroom, brushed my teeth, scowled at my sleep-ridden appearance, and headed to the kitchen. "Man, you look bad," Ian said as I passed by.

"I know, I couldn't sleep."

"Aw. Nightmares?" He teased in a childish voice.

"No." I laughed. "I was working."

"Oh really?"

"I think I might have something today," I said as I walked and crammed a granola bar into my mouth.

—

The hormone was injected into my body. My heart raced and my skin pricked with excitement as I knew what I was about to get myself into.

When I entered, I was not taken to Ethan's body right away. Instead, everything remained black. I panicked, and as I stood suspended in the air, five blue orbs floated toward me, then circled me. The blue lights touched my skin like soft kisses. I stared in amazement, and the more I stared, I realized they had no idea how much pain and torture was headed their way. I want them to remain the way they are; I want to protect them from this cruel place we have all had to endure.

A plethora of blue orbs appeared until there were hundreds of them. *I don't understand, what is happen—*

Ethan walked toward me. *He's never come to me before, I always come to him.* His face was peaceful, and even through the many wounds, he looked exhilarated. The blue light of a nearby orb crept across the right side of his face as he slowly took a slight turn to the left.

"Where are you ..." I thought he was about to walk in a different direction.

His eyes gave me a cue to look straight.

In the distance, two tiny figures appeared. As I tried to focus my eyes on the figures, I was abruptly taken to them. Just like when I enter the pre-birth world and I am taken to "my" body fighting. I looked around me and saw Ethan by my side, along with the hundreds of blue orbs that circled above and around us. I put my attention back on the figures I was brought to; they were people. One dark-skinned tall boy and another strikingly familiar young man.

"Is that—"

"That's you," Ethan said. "This was your first fight."

Chapter 6

I let out a sound that was between a sigh of relief and a small laugh. As I examined myself (it felt amazing to finally say that), I had a few scratches here and there and I got repeatedly knocked down by a few strong punches from my opponent.

I looked tired and weak, then I remembered what Ethan said. *I watched you fight and you barely made it out.* It seemed that no matter how many times I tried to stand up, I was pushed back down. My opponent beat me, adding my crimson blood to stain the floor. This continued for some time and I grew tempted to turn away.

Then, not long after that, I had my opponent in a headlock before I snapped his neck, leaving a cold lifeless body on the floor. I watched myself stare at him. Everything went black, as if someone turned off a power generator, but Ethan still stood by my side. "That was … odd," I said in a daze.

"Wasn't for me," he said with a laugh. "I've watched you win that fight repeatedly for years. I'm just glad I don't have to be jealous of your success anymore."

"What do you mean 'you don't have to anymore'?"

"I always see you fighting, you and about half the people in here never take a break when the rest of us only fight twice a day, and you all are repeatedly fighting the same person. Even though you were born, for some reason your soul never stops fighting." *The people he referred to are souls that have already won. They kept fighting because the connection with the DNA had never been made to end the fight.*

Just to clarify my theory, I added, "You never answered my question. What did you mean when you said you don't have to see me anymore?"

"I mean I don't see you fighting right now, which is something that has never happened before. I assumed that I won't be seeing you anymore," he said nonchalantly. I was lost in thought for a moment, and when I came back to my reality, it's like I had been slapped in the face. There was so much going on before that I had not realized his odd appearance. It's not odd in a bad way, he just looked different. His skin had a bit more color to it and he seemed to stand straighter. He took note of the look on my face and tried to guess its origin. "You have to head back now, right?" I do, but I am expected to return to R.B. with something they can use. *What can I tell them?*

"You will tell them to collect the DNA from the souls in the pre-birth world and then we can mix it with the matching DNA of a member from your society," my brother interjected.

I forgot that Ethan could hear my thoughts.

I opened my mouth to tell Ethan what a great idea this was when we were swiftly taken to Ethan's new opponent, a boy in a wheelchair. Visible cuts and scrapes peered out from his tousled brown hair with dried blood in it. He wore a dark-green shirt filled with rips and holes, his arms covered in oozing bite marks.

Ethan seemed as if he didn't know where to hit him, and as always, he hesitated. The boy took this to his advantage. He stood with shaking legs, jumped on Ethan, and they beat each other for an endless amount of time. The boy pulled out a knife and held it to Ethan's throat.

Why does everyone in here seem to have a weapon but my brother!

"They aren't available to me for some reason!" he yelled back in my head. Ethan clutched the boy's forearms to push the knife away from his face, his hands slipped off the boy's arms and made the knife shake violently. The boy's grip loosened on the knife and it fell out of his hands. He reached behind him to retrieve it. I ran up to Ethan. "Put your hand on my arm!"

"Really? Right now?"

"Yes, I need his blood!" He stared at me, confused, and the vein in my forehead started to twitch like it was going to burst any second. "Hurry up!"

47

He placed his hand, covered in the boy's blood, on my arm. The boy grabbed the wheelchair by its wheels, lifted it over his head, and threw it as hard as he could on top of Ethan. The handle of the chair plunged into Ethan's eye, squishing it like a grape. The sound of it made me cringe and the sound of Ethan's scream filled the darkness. As he died, his body disappeared and so did the boy in the wheelchair. The only thing I had left of the fight was a messy smear of the boy's blood on my arm.

When Ethan returned to me, I expected him to gasp for air and struggle, but he didn't. There were a few staggered breaths here and there, but his voice regained strength.

"I'll see you tomorrow," I told him as I felt the blood dry on my arm.

"Okay."

I disconnected and my mind slipped away from this strange world I'd become accustomed to.

Chapter 7

"Hey," Ian said as he looked down at me from where I lay in the cot. The overhead light above his head made green-and-blue spots appear in my vision. "Did we get anything?" The fact that he said *we* made my stomach jolt. *"We" did not get anything. I got* *something because I'm the one doing all the work.* "I got something." I corrected him and paused to collect myself.

"Well?"

"Ian, I've told you a million times. I need a second to adjust my eyes."

"What'd you get?" Paul said eagerly.

I'm going to wring your neck! I wanted to scream but I bit my tongue. "I figured out how to see myself and I know how to let others see themselves."

"You really saw yourself? You're positive?"

I took a calming breath and said in a monotone voice, "Yes, Paul. I saw myself," and a huge smile appeared on his face. He took out a pen and paper as his hands shook with excitement.

"Well, elaborate a little. How did you figure all this out?" I couldn't really tell him *how*, so I cut to the chase.

I told him about mixing the DNA of the souls together. "Why is there blood on your arm?" he interrupted. "This is blood from a rival soul. We need to take it in for testing, figure out whose blood this is in real life, then go find that person and get a sample of their blood. Then, we need to mix the two samples together. When this is done, the person will be able to see their soul." A deep crease formed between his brows as he meticulously wrote the information down. "I need you to start from the beginning. How did you figure all of this out?"

"I-I just figured it out."

"Yes, I understand that. How?"

"It's … complicated. But I figured it out, that's all that matters, right?"

"Jacob, what have you not been telling us?" he yelled in my face. The room was spinning, my heart was pounding, and I felt like I had an elephant on my chest. I can't let them know about Ethan. I had to protect him and help him win before they could know of his existence. If Paul knew I could communicate with Ethan, he would use him to his advantage. I'd already left Ethan abandoned, alone, and defenseless. I can't exploit him in this unforgiving world. I had to protect my brother. I was breathing heavily and beads of sweat ran down my face as I began to overthink the situation.

"Paul, give him some space. He doesn't look too good," Ian said from the back of the room. "I'll take him to get the blood tested. Then I'll take him to his room so he can rest." After a long moment of silence, Paul mumbled, "Fine," and he stepped away from the cot.

Later, I sat in a chair while Ian swabbed my blood-stained arm with a cotton swab. "Look at all of this," Michael said from the room across the hall.

"What are those?" Ian said as he looked down at nearly a dozen envelopes, half of them read.

"Mail, from the society, and they are all addressed to Paul." Michael picked up one unread envelope, tore it open, and read its contents.

"It's from a girl named Ren. She wants to become a volunteer tester, like Jacob."

"They are all volunteering to be testers," Ian said as he examined the mail. "Some of them are adults and some of them are teenagers. In the past few days, they have been coming like wildfire." This can't be going over well with society leaders. They kicked me out for having favored the thought of R.B. and "disrupting the peace." I can't imagine what they would do if they found out that a handful of people asked to be a part of R.B.

Everything was silent until Ian swabbed my arm. "Don't let Paul make you feel like you have to rush with your process. He's just irritated because things aren't happening as fast as he would like them to."

I was about to say something when he cut me off. "But ... we all know that there is something you are not telling us. I know that you might not want to share with the group everything you see in there, but things aren't looking too great for you right now."

"What do you mean?"

"Paul has never trusted you, and right now, you're giving him more of a reason not to."

"Why has he never trusted me? What did I ever do to make him not?"

"You ..." It sounded like he might have held back the truth. "You didn't do anything. It's just because ... you're from the society."

"So, the fact that I left my life to come and help the cause makes me untrustworthy? Even though I am the reason why this project is still going. He *still* doesn't trust me?"

He looked me dead in the eye and said, "Jacob, do you have any idea of how much power you have? You are the only person in our team who has ever seen the pre-birth world. We have no idea of what is going on in there, and when you are in there for hours at a time, how could he not get a little suspicious?" He brought the cotton swab over to a machine to collect the DNA.

I sighed and said, "Look, the only thing I can do to make him happy is to collect blood samples from the souls that I see. In no time, we should have enough DNA to match it with a small group from the society." Ian didn't respond right away because he was too busy typing away on the machine.

Come to think of it, I didn't think he was listening to me. "Come here for a second, this doesn't make sense to me,"

"What are you talking about?"

"The DNA from the soul, it's a match to Aaron Parker's DNA."

"And?"

"Aaron was born two hours ago."

Chapter 8

"Jacob, I don't think I fully understand this. I thought you told us that the person would be able to see himself in the pre-birth world."

What are you talking about? "I did and he will."

"But, he's an infant. How will we be able to see if this works?"

But it does work. It worked for me!

"We will wait until he's older." I hesitated.

"Have you not been listening this entire time? Paul wants an answer right now! How do you even know this will work?"

"I told you. I got my soul's blood on my shirt the first time. Then we matched the blood. It does work."

Ian looked down at the floor. His lips started to move but no sound came out. "This is what I mean! Nothing you are saying is adding up!"

"What are you talking about?" I said with defense.

"You always told us that you could never see your soul without having a blood sample."

"That's true. What's your point?"

"If you could never see your soul initially, how did you get the blood in the first place?" The sound of Ian's voice seemed to increase with every word. Naturally, the staff members crowded around the door to see what all the fuss was about.

"See, this is why Paul doesn't trust you, you never give us the whole story! We have been working day and night. We have dedicated our lives to this project and you're over here keeping secrets. Guess this is what we get for hiring a kid."

"So now this is about my age? We are the same age, Ian! I deserve to be here just as much as you do!"

"You don't deserve any of this! I have been working to get this position my entire life. I grew up in this. You're just a nobody from the society who was bored one day. You hardly know anything about this stuff."

"I just found someone who I saw in the pre-birth world. I'm doing everything we wanted." I motioned to the screen with my hand.

"Yes, I know that, but Aaron is a dead end, it will take years before he is ready."

"Well, I'll go back in and get another blood sample."

"No, you won't," Paul chimed in. I looked at him with pure confusion on my face and I felt that our conversation would not be pleasant. "You're off the team, Jacob. Gather your things and get out."

"Paul ..."

"Ian's right, you're too unprofessional for this job."

His eyes were cold; he had been waiting a long time to do this. "You'll be out by morning."

"So that's it? Just going to toss me out into the streets?"

"Got any better ideas?" he asked heartlessly.

—

When I woke up in the morning, all my belongings were in a black trash bag that sat slumped over in the corner. I made my way to the kitchen only to find Paul, who stood stiffly at the entrance. "What do you think you're doing?"

"Getting breakfast, or can you not trust me?" I snapped.

"You don't live here anymore. This isn't your food to take."

"Do you know how ridiculous you're being right now?"

"Just get out of here. I'm sick of you wasting our time and resources," he said as he pushed my shoulders. His back bumped the door and it opened slightly, where Ian sat alone at the oval table eating an apple. We held each other's gaze until he broke it by looking at the floor.

As I walked down the hallway, I heard someone running behind me. I whipped around, expecting to see Paul, but was surprised to see a girl with long brown hair running at me. Her footsteps are light, as if she ran on a cloud.

"Here," she said, handing me a granola bar. Her green eyes held my gaze for a moment.

"Who are you?" I asked.

"I'm Ren. The new tester."

"Thought you might want some breakfast before you go," she said before she walked back down the hallway, to take my job, my life, and the pre-birth world right out of my hands.

Chapter 9

I felt jealous, and the emotion filled my entire body. I hate having known that I was so easy to replace. My rage-filled eyes seemed to simmer down when I looked and saw that she got my favorite granola bar. It made me feel slightly better about her.

I took a bite and pushed open the heavy metal door, stepping out into the summer air. Blocking the blinding sun with my forearm, I pushed the sleeves on my white shirt up to my elbows while I bit the inside of my lip, thinking about where I was going to go. I decided to go into the "decent" part of the city.

Two miles later, I was pouring sweat and my black trash bag was scolding hot from the sun. I was in the city, but I was not where I needed to be yet. I walked to the small blue bus station and collapsed on the bench. I brushed some dirt off my left shoulder and realized I was sitting beside a man covered in soot. He turned his head to the right, and we stared at each other for one painfully long second.

"Nice bag," he said in a raspy voice while he motioned his head down to the bag at my feet. I nodded awkwardly. "I would start watching my back if I were you, son." I gave him a funny look. "Oh, but I won't tell anyone.

It'll be our little secret," he said with a wink. Thank goodness the bus pulled up. The whole situation was bizarre. I pushed it out of my mind and tried to focus my attention on where I was headed next.

I climbed up the steps and walked over to a seat, only to find that my new "friend," planned to sit across from me. I looked forward to him and he flashed a toothy yellow smile at me. *You're creepy as hell, dude.* I sat in a seat between two middle-aged women. Every now and then, I saw the man giving me a sad look from across the bus. My eyes wandered to all the ads that lined the border of the bus. I didn't think much of them until I saw a collage of faces with names printed under them. At the top, it said: **WANTED**, then it showed eleven unfamiliar faces and names. The tenth face was familiar: *Ren Hedrick*. The photo of the girl pictured was identical to the green-eyed girl who gave me the granola bar. The new tester.

Why is she on a flyer? Does R.B. know who they hired? That proves how thoughtless Paul is, he can't even perform a proper background check on someone. She won't last two weeks, I bet. I laughed to myself.

As I looked at the other nine faces lining the bus wall, I tried to hide a smile about my discovery of the girl when I noticed the next face plastered on the wall. All the emotion I had ripped away.

Jacob Sims. The poster read.

A wave of nausea crashed inside my body.

Why am I wanted? How did they get this picture? At the bottom of the poster, it read: ***All eleven wanted for disrupting the peace. $10,000 will be awarded if any are turned in.***

At that moment, I remembered that R.B. was sent eleven letters, all who asked if they could be a tester. These are the people who wrote these, and I am the one who left the society. I looked at the people around me and panic filled my body. Any one of them could realize who I am and turn me in.

Is this what the man meant? He said he wouldn't tell anyone … That it was our secret.

At the next stop, I followed the crowd and I thought I might get off without anyone recognizing me, until I went down the steps and my trash bag accidentally hit the bus driver's shoulder.

"Sorry sir," I said while I tried to keep my head down.

"It's fine." I was about to continue walking when he said, "Wait, do I know you?"

"No, you must think I'm someone else."

"No … I do know you." He looked down for half a second. "You're that guy from the poster! The wanted poster!" he said, pointing to the poster beside him. He pulled out his phone, and I pushed the people out of the way to get off the bus.

"Don't move!" he screamed behind me as I ran down the street, in the opposite direction. I passed an unchained bike on a bike rack and hopped on it. I silently apologized to whoever's bike it was. I rode at least two miles and I was sure that the bus driver was no longer behind me. I checked, to be sure. I saw no sign of him and felt a rush of adrenaline surge through me. A horn blared in front of me. When I turned my head back to the road, a red car was inches away from hitting me.

"Hey! Watch it!" a pedestrian yelled, then looked at me closer through the windshield.

"You're him! You're that guy!" he yelled as he swung open the car door and ran toward me. "The cops know you're here! I want ten grand for turning you in!" I pedaled as fast as I could down the street. He was a few feet behind me and I panicked. There was a crowd of people to the right, and I figured I could lose the man if I went into it. I threw the bike down and weaved my way through, and eventually, I lost him. I ran off the side street and met the edge of the woods, then hiked one of the many hills.

The trees were full and green, and I took in their beauty until I got too occupied swatting the many flies off my body. I'd have to go into the city at night to get food, but for now, I looked for an area where I could make a camp. When I looked to the east, the ground was flatter and less rocky. I set up camp there under a large tree. Sitting on the dry soil with my back against the tree, I rubbed my aching feet. R.B.'s building barely poked through the trees. The building sat on a side street apart from the city, where not many people go anymore. I was about a mile away.

"Jacob!" Ethan screamed inside my head. I didn't expect this, and it made me jump.

"Ethan? What's wrong?"

"Where the hell have you been? I've been looking for you all day." I didn't respond for a while. "Jacob, what the hell is going on? Why are you—"

"I can't come see you anymore," I blurted out.

"What? What are you talking about?"

"I'm … not able to go into your world anymore."

"But how am I supposed to get out of here?" His voice sounded so hurt and vulnerable. "I'm not strong enough."

"Yes, you are, I can see it. Your body looks stronger, you are fighting better every day. You don't need my help, you can do this all on your own."

"Jacob I-I …"

"This is your fight to win, you are ready." I actually had no idea if he was ready. It was a total jerk move, but I needed to think about how I was going to help *myself*.

"Jacob, please!"

"Ethan," I said sternly. "Man up, do it yourself. I'm not going to hold your hand through this anymore. I just got myself in a ton of trouble. I'm in a bad situation right now and this is too much for me! It's your fight, not mine!"

"So, I'm not trying hard enough?" he yelled. "Do you think I just sit around here for hours daydreaming? Just waiting for someone to come and *free* me?"

"That's exactly what I think you are doing. You are putting so much pressure on me to get you out and I have tried everything!" I paused for a moment, and I contemplated what I was going to say next. As soon as I said it, I wished I contemplated it for a moment more.

"If you can't win this next fight … I don't know, maybe you were never meant to be born."

"Jacob … I'm your brother."

"Are you?"

Gosh, I hate myself.

Chapter 10

I was alone in the dark woods. I was freezing and I had lost my appetite for food. All because of what I said to Ethan. I stared up at the stars and cringed at how mean I was to him. He was my responsibility and I felt terrible that I let him go, but what more could I do? I can't see him anymore. I do not have access to R.B. or the antidote. Maybe I was right, maybe I was never meant to have a twin.

I stared down at R.B. from my place on the hill and I thought about how simple everything used to be. How simple everything was before I knew about Ethan.

Paul was nicer when I first volunteered. We had just started R.B. and we knew as a team, we could support each other. Together, we were a family but then Paul let the stress of the project get to him and the warmth of our team became cold.

A small plane flew over my head. I watched it pass by. It was so low that it nearly touched the treetops. It flew over R.B. and I didn't think much of it until it opened a door, and dropped something on the building. The world seemed to stop for half a second until it was disrupted by the explosion of a bomb.

The entire far right side of the building no longer existed, and the rest of the building was ignited in flames. A pit formed in the bottom of my stomach as I imagined the sound of their screams.

My team was in there!

I should have felt nothing but hatred toward them, but they were my family and R.B. was my home for so many years. The plane flew into the distance, leaving a smoky sky illuminated by the fire behind it.

I sprang to a standing position. My heart beat rapidly as I contemplated what to do next. I trained my eyes on the now crumbling building and debated whether I should help.

Before I knew it, I ran toward the site. R.B. was a part of who I was and full of innocent people who needed my help, including Ian, my team, and the only access I have to the pre-birth world to see Ethan.

Suddenly, my thoughts were interrupted by Ren's picture from the poster. She was not like the others; she was from the society, searching for answers and a new life, just like I was, like I *am*. She was not one of them; she didn't belong there, and that's why I had to go and help her. *It's only a few miles,* I told myself as I ran down the hill. I stumbled over fallen tree branches, and the unruly grass whipped my shins as I ran through it.

I glanced to my left at R.B. The fire had spread to the field behind it and the vacant alley around the area was blown to bits. I needed to get everyone, especially Ren, out of there. Unsure if I felt this way because I wanted to redeem myself for leaving my brother defenseless. However, I knew I had a connection to this stranger of a girl.

I was only a few feet away when pieces of drywall fell from the ceiling. They landed on the center of the bookcase, which caught on fire and made beads of sweat race down my face. Ren lay under the bookcase on her back, only a thin piece of wood kept her face from burning off. I hoped to get there before that happened.

The building only had two walls left and the rest would come tumbling down at any moment. I grabbed the corner of the bookcase and carefully lifted it off her. Ash covered her body while the gash on the side of her head left red streaks down her cheeks. As I gathered her in my arms, someone ran into the building.

"What the hell happened?" Paul yelled as he looked around. He didn't even notice me, unlike the fire and the debris, which made his eyes become ridden with panic. Then, his face went white, his eyes went blank, and he ran to the cabinets in front of me. He swung the doors open and rummaged through its contents while he muttered words under his breath. "No, no, no, no. This can't be happening. It's all gone."

"What is it, Paul?" Michael asked in a frightened tone.

Paul spun around to face him. He had a crazed look in his eyes; he didn't even look human.

"The hormone, you idiot! We have no more! We can't ..." He slammed the cabinet door shut.

"Paul, calm down. We can make more! We have to get out of here. Now!" Michael coughed.

"Do you have any idea how long that will take? Do you?"

"It—"

"Shut up! Just shut up!" Paul screamed.

The ceiling above Ren and me gave away and came crashing down. Thankfully, we were able to escape in time although I can't say the same for Paul. The cabinets fell on top of him and the glass vials fell all around him. We stood in the middle of the floor, and I looked at my surroundings to try and find a way out. I could easily escape out of the exposed wall in front of me, but the entrance was ignited with fire. The door on the opposite side of the building could work. I turned around and stared down the smoke-filled hallway as the lights flickered. I ran down the hallway with Ren's limp body in my arms. I saw the exit as I passed the kitchen, but something made me stop in my tracks. The room was filled with debris from the wall that fell, a fire grew in the back corner, and the refrigerator lay on the broken floor. What caught my eye was the blood oozing out from underneath the refrigerator and a shrilling voice.

"Jacob! Plea-please help me! M-my legs! Help me!" Ian pleaded breathlessly. The refrigerator had crushed his legs. I didn't know what to do. Even if I could get him out, he would be paralyzed, and he wouldn't live long. Ren was still unconscious and I couldn't carry them both.

"Jacob! Please." His voice quivered as he started to cry. "I-I know I was a jerk to you. I'm sorry!"

"Ian, I—"

"Don't you dare say you can't do this! Don't you dare leave me here!" he yelled through coughs. I looked at Ren and I laid her gently down on the floor. I tried to lift the refrigerator, but it was too heavy and I couldn't breathe. It was too smokey, I couldn't see. The fire spread and softly touched Ian's skin. He screamed as it covered his body. I couldn't think, I couldn't look away. The smoke made me lightheaded and dizzy as my eyelids grew heavy. I was helpless, thinking there was no way out and I couldn't save my friend, until she coughed.

Get it together Jacob!

I pulled my shirt over my nose, swung her over my shoulder, and went back into the hallway to look for an exit.

There's nowhere I can go!

The ceiling rumbled, threatening to come down.

We're trapped! You waited too long!

The kitchen, hallway, and the lab were all completely on fire but there was still the sleeping unit that was in the front of the building. I ran to it and stepped over fallen furniture. I pushed open the window and jumped out onto the pavement.

Chapter 11

I lay on my side and gasped for air as Ren slowly opened her eyes. Her face had streaks from soot and she had a terrible cough. The sounds of the fire crackled behind me and I feared the building would collapse. I picked Ren up with my weak arms and moved us down the street, safe from the fire. I placed her on the pavement.

"Jacob, what—" She interrupted herself as she winced and grabbed her side, which caused her to hunch over.

"What is it?" I said, alarmed, and knelt beside her. She yelped in pain. "Ren? Talk to me. What's happening?"

"My stomach." She winced, her eyes shut tight. She lifted her shirt slightly. Revealing that the right side of her torso has been scorched by the fire.

"You were burned pretty badly. We need to get you something for that."

"No, we don't. I'm fine. I'm not going into the city just so that I can be arrested."

"Ren, it's still dark out. We can go get some medical supplies. We'll be out of the city in no time."

"No, I—"

"If you pass out or something, I'm the one who's going to have to carry you around and I'm not entirely up for that. So, we are going,"

"Jacob," she said in a high-pitched voice. "If we do this, how are we going to get there? We are miles away from the city." She had a point. If we were to walk, it might become daylight before we could leave unseen.

I thought about this for a minute and then said, "R.B. has a van. We can use that if it's still intact. Paul was driving it just before the explosion happened, so let's hope it's safe." The van was parked not far from where we stood. We walked down the smoky, dimly lit street until we approached the white van. "Now, we just need the … keys," which were with one of the assistants back in the building.

Ren looked at me with a puzzled expression. "Are you an idiot? You're not thinking about going back into a burning building?" she teased.

"We need—"

"I can hot-wire it, just show me where the van is."

Who is this girl?

"How the hell does a girl like you know how to hotwire a car?" I chuckled.

"You barely even know me." Her voice sparked something inside of me. I saw all the small details about her. The way a lock of her dark hair softly brushed along the side of her cheek. The crease between her brows as she meticulously worked on the car. How her hands seemed to glide through the air as if she were weightless.

"I'm about done," she said after a while. Beads of sweat threatened to fall from her hairline. Her face was pink and she kept flipping her hair out of her eyes vigorously. It may be because of smoke inhalation but her distress amused me and I chuckled.

"What?" she said, halfway yelling at me.

"If you can't do it, we can find another—"

"No, I almost have it. Why do you think that I can't do this?"

"I never said I didn't think you could." I laughed. The lightheartedness of the conversation seemed to help both of us feel better about the experience we had.

"Look. I'm done. We can go now," she said in a monotone voice, and I remained puzzled by her attitude. "Come on," she said as she climbed into the passenger seat.

"Are you okay?"

"No, I'm not Jacob."

"Why not? Why are you angry with me all of a sudden?"

"Because Jacob, I just almost died in a burning building and now you're hauling me off into the city, which I didn't even want to do in the first place."

"What, did you want to lay down in bed while I waited on your hand and foot?"

"No, I—"

"I don't have time for that. If you don't like this arrangement, then you shouldn't be here." I turned the corners of the old, abandoned road. The sky had become gray as the sun threatened to rise. I couldn't put the headlights on because I didn't want to risk unwanted attention. That made it difficult to see where I was going. The smoke in the sky became denser as we reached the city, which didn't make any sense because R.B.'s bombed building was miles behind.

"I shouldn't be here? I never asked you to come and help me …"

I directed my attention to the glowing, orange hue that peeked out through the trees ahead of us. In the middle of the fiery trees lay the city, and I felt my stomach drop.

Chapter 12

I floored the gas pedal before Ren
had time to finish her sentence, making
her gasp loudly. "What the hell, Jacob!"
she yelled. "Is that—"

"Fire? Yes."

"What's going on?"

"I don't know. That's why I am trying to get up there."

She had started to irritate me at this point.

"Look," I said as I pulled into a clearing to see what was going on. My eyes widened as I saw what was in front of me. The city was a madhouse. Shops and houses were ablaze with fire as citizens ran up and down the streets screaming. On another street, a mob of people came marching up the street, holding picket signs mentioning something about R.B. Some of them had pictures of people shown on the wanted list. As I read more of the signs, I realized that these people were not protesting against R.B., they were supporting it. Other picket signs even mentioned things that are wrong with our society and how it was unfair that R.B. was being ridiculed for what it stood for. The people not protesting threw broken beer bottles at them and attacked them.

"R.B. doesn't follow our religious values!" one of the protesters screamed.

"The pre-birth world has nothing to do with faith or religion! R.B. is showing us the truth!" the other protesters yelled back.

"It isn't right!" a pedestrian screamed. "Those are our sons and daughters! What kind of person would support this?"

Negative energy thickened the air as many arguments began to arise from the mob. "My daughter wants to be one of them, it's disgusting! I can't believe this is happening to us!" A blonde woman said to her friend right before a man with an untrimmed beard yelled in her face.

"You people are so close-minded! You don't know where we come from! How can you say that about your daughter?"

"She's not my daughter anymore," the blonde woman yelled over a roar of many angry voices. "Now that she is going to hell!"

"What does that have to do with anything?" the man yelled as his face reddens.

"God is where we came from! Not this 'pre-birth world' nonsense they try to make us believe! This isn't how things are supposed to be! It's not realistic!"

"No one is trying to *make* you believe anything, it's just a theory!" he said as they continued to bicker with each other. There must have been a more heated argument in the back of the crowd because the sound of a gunshot echoed through the streets and only the sound of a crackling fire could be heard. The sudden screams from the people almost seemed to illuminate the dark sky, as if the shrill sounds shook it awake. Many people fled the scene, but one huddle of men remained. Ren and I watch them as they meet their fists to each other's faces. The fire contained in the blue house up the street spread onto the front lawn, then it eventually combined with the fire that swallowed the neighboring house.

A small crowd of people ran by our car and one man stopped in front of it and said, "Hey, it's them!" and pointed to our faces. "Those two kids from the poster!" People crowded around our car, some looked hopeful, some looked furious and outraged, but they all started shouting at the same time.

"Do you know where my daughter is? Her name is Abby!" said the muffled voice of a lady in the back of the crowd. I can barely hear her over all the commotion. "She has been missing for—"

"Drive!" Ren yelled beside me. I hit the gas, not caring if I hit anyone in front of me.

"Stop!" a man yelled as he gripped the car window frame. "This is all your fault. Our society would be at peace if you kept your unwanted theories to yourself!" He grabbed my shirt, trying to pull me out of the car.

"Let go of him!" a pedestrian yelled as he tackled the man to the ground. I pressed harder on the gas pedal and I thought that we just might make it out until someone threw a rock at our windshield. The rock broke the glass, which made it resemble a spider web. Ren screamed and our car swerved.

My vision kept going black, then it flashed back to the road and went black again. I couldn't seem to keep focused and I felt lightheaded. *Get it together, Jacob. You have to focus. Focus.*

I nearly drove off the road, so hot I thought I was about to be sick. "Jacob!" Ren yelled in a scolding voice. Everything sounded muffled as if I were underwater and my ears rang. It went black again, but this time, something was different. I was looking through someone else's eyes. As chills ran up my arms, I realized this all too familiar sensation the first time Ethan had reached out to me from the pre-birth world. I looked closely into the darkness. Ahead I saw the faint silhouette of a boy. As I began to seek out the details of his face, "I" lunged forward, wrapped my arms around his neck, and twisted it in one quick movement. I had no idea what was going on or why, but I felt so confident in this moment; it was second nature to me.

As soon as I heard the snap of his neck, a white light flashed in my face. The light ignited all the darkness that surrounded me, and for once in my life, I felt complete, weightless, and refreshed.

"Are you okay?" Ren asked, shaking me with a crazed look in her eyes. I didn't respond right away, too busy trying to wrap my head around what I saw.

It can't be …

Ren has been steering the car the entire time I was out. "Are you okay?" she asked again.

"He will be here," I said above a whisper, although I meant to say it just to myself.

"I didn't hear what you said. Can you say it again?" she asked as she quickly turned her head to look at me.

"He will be here." A small smile crept onto my face. I can't believe I get to say this. Ethan won his first fight and now he is here, with me, somewhere in this world. All I had to do was find him when the time came.

"Who will be here? What happened to you?"

"My—" *How do I even put this?* "I-I … don't know. We just need to get out of here."

How do I know that he will be born? What if I imagined it?

I had no answer.

I couldn't afford to think about "what if" and willed myself to have faith that my brother would be here with me, in this dimension.

—

We drove for a few miles and escaped the protesters chasing us. We ended up on a deserted highway, unsure of where we were headed, but we needed to stay near the city to stay tuned into what was happening. As we drove down the open road with nothing to accompany us but the light of the moon and the sound of the howling wind, I understood how alone Ren and I were in this close-minded world. We are outcasts, looked over by society. When in reality, we are the ones who should be looked up to. We are the ones that hold the secret to the origin of human beings.

Into the distance, the silhouette of a cement bridge stood as if it were a symbol of our salvation. It was far enough from the city to where we could not be seen but close enough to where the city lights were still visible: the perfect place for us to stay for a little while. "Pull off here and stop under that bridge," I said.

"Why?"

"So we can set up camp."

"Is it safe?" she asked as she turned her head toward me and the moonlight cast a shadow on the left side of her face.

"Ren … anywhere we go isn't going to be safe." I chuckled.

Below the cement bridge was damp and cold. A mysterious liquid spewed on the ground and I didn't want to begin to assume what it may be. Fragments of half-eaten food and candy wrappers formed a trail to the dark corner on the right. Someone had been sleeping here.

Chapter 13

It was nine months later and the sun was beginning to rise. Ren and I had come up with a decent weekly routine in the past nine months. Every Sunday morning, we would go to the market to get the supplies we needed for the week and during the weekdays we would both work odd jobs from anyone who would have the heart to hire us. Supporters of R.B. were always willing to let us mow their lawns or attend to their gardens. With the money Ren and I would both earn we barely had enough to buy our necessities.

—

We decided to go into the city to get supplies for the week. I could see the skyscrapers from the city standing tall and proud. Here and there, waves of smoke from a dying fire drifted into the sky. The four large screens that broadcast the daily news are now shattered due to objects being thrown at them by the protesters. Some of the screens have turned green and started to quiver with static while one flickered on and off as it tried to project a message. Black letters appeared on the left side of the screen and I could briefly make out the name "Thomas." Under it, it read:

"Born August 5, 2523, at 2:06 a.m."

I questioned why this would be on the screen until I remembered that our society does this for the first child born every month.

The time captivated my attention for a moment as I tried to piece together *our* life: 2:06 a.m. It was currently 5:42 a.m. I then thought about nine months ago when I had my vision. Ethan should have been born this month, and so was Thomas.

Is it?

My thoughts were interrupted when the right half of the screen flickered back on and revealed further information about Thomas's birth.

"At Richardson's Memorial Hospital, all visitors are welcome."

This was my chance to make things right, this was my chance to be a part of my brother's life. The only question was, would *they* allow it? Ethan has his own family now; he is no longer mine. I can't even say that he is my twin anymore considering I am twenty-two years older than him. The reality of this hit me like a brick and my stomach felt unsettled. I had lost him. Even though he was in the same city as me, he felt further away than ever.

"What's wrong? You look worried," Ren asked as she touched my arm. I let out a sigh, not knowing where to begin. Ren didn't know who Ethan was. I never got a chance to tell her. Seizing the moment, I told her the story of my brother. The closer I got to the end, the deeper the line between her brows formed. After a long moment of silence, she looked at me with questionable eyes. "Why aren't we driving to the hospital right now?" she asked, taking my hand and pulling me into the car.

I thought I was in shock. I lost the one person who I felt the strongest connection to, and it pained me to think about how likely it was that I'd never get the bond I had with him back. He would never be able to remember the pre-birth world.

The hospital was only a few miles away, and in no time, we were there. As I opened the door to get out of the car, Ren pulled me back. "Here, put these on. We can't let them recognize us." She handed me a pair of old sunglasses.

I doubt that this will prevent us from being recognized but at least it's something.

As we walked through the clean glass doors of the hospital, I noticed all the people in the waiting room with wounds. Some of them were protesters who got hurt in the riots. We walked up to the front desk and the receptionist asked us how she could help us. I hesitate before I revert my attention to the floor. "We are here to pay our respects to Eth ... Thomas," I said with a swift correction.

"What's the last name?"

I panicked. I didn't know his last name. She looked at me with a blank stare and opened her mouth to say something. "Thomas was the first child born this month?"

"Yes."

She clicked away at her computer screen. "We are friends of the family," I added.

"Alright. Room 308 on the third floor." I headed toward the elevators until I was stopped in my tracks. "Oh, and Jacob. Good luck."

"What?" I asked as I swiftly turned around.

"It's okay. You don't have to hide here."

"I don't know what you are talking about."

"Everyone here at the hospital are your supporters. You are safe here. It's out there that you have to worry about. It's okay. Go do whatever it is that you need to do."

My skin became hot.

Don't trust her. She's going to turn you in. Get out of here now.

I almost listened to my gut but something inside me told me to let my guard down. I came here for him. I came here to see him, and nothing can jeopardize that.

We ran to the elevator, pressed the button with the number three on it, and urged the doors to close. After a minute of painful silence between Ren and me, the silver doors finally slid open. We exchanged nervous glances as we walked onto the floor booming with new life. I didn't know where to go. Should I ask someone and risk being turned in? Or had the lady told the truth when she said that we were safe here? I decided not to risk it and walked straight ahead. Nurses swarmed around the halls like it was a beehive.

Ren headed down the hallway to my right without giving me any notice. "What are you doing?" I hissed.

"What are *you* doing?" She laughed. "Start looking around," she hissed back. "Room 308 should be around here somewhere."

We walked for a short distance until we rounded a corner. I nearly missed running into a male nurse who was walking in the opposite direction. He gave a half smile as he walked past me, and that's when I saw it, the newborn nursery. The sun reflected off of its glass window, giving it a warm and youthful glow. Ren led the way to room 308, but as we walked past the nursery, a weird sensation took hold of me, like for once in my life I was not alone, and guided me to the window.

"Jacob?" Ren whispered sincerely. She took another breath to talk, but I held a finger up to my lips. I scanned the clipboards on the cribs, looking for the name Thomas. I started to think he was back in his room until my eyes reverted to the last crib in the back row. "*Thomas Whitman,*" the clipboard read. The world felt like it stopped spinning to give all of its attention to this moment, this miracle. My heart skipped a beat.

That's him. That's my twin. He looked just like I did when I was a baby. Brown hair, ivory skin, a straight thin nose, heart-shaped lips, and his eyes don't fully close when he sleeps, just like mine.

My intense staring was suddenly disrupted when a nurse walked in. She went straight to Thomas, took a look at his chart, and wheeled him out the door.

Where is she taking him? "What is she doing?" The crease between my eyebrows deepens.

"It's okay. She's just taking him back to his room. Come on," Ren whispers. We walked a safe distance behind the blonde nurse as she took the next left.

Eventually, she wheeled him to room 308 while we pretended to buy something from the vending machine. She shut the door behind her and we eavesdropped outside of the door. For about fifteen minutes, Thomas's parents only talked about baby things and how lucky they were. Ren had an annoying smile on her face.

"I think he looks like your brother," the father said.

"I see more of your dad," the mother replied.

"Hm."

"What?" She laughed before an awkward moment of silence.

"This is our kid, right?" he whispered hesitantly.

"Tom!" I heard her slap him, on the arm I assume. "Why would you say that? Of course, he is ours!"

"I'm sorry Caroline, just ... I can't really ... We are both part Native American."

"If you think that you're not the father Tom—"

"No, no, I'm not saying that, of course, I'm not. I know you wouldn't do something like that. I was just making a comment." There is a moment of silence, and I could feel her heated eyes glare at him as if he were a piece of meat.

"Do you need anything? I need to use the restroom. I can stop by the cafeteria while I'm gone if you want," Tom asked his wife before the door quickly opened, leaving us no time to make our escape. Tom bumped into me as he turned to the left.

"What are you doing here?" he asked in a deep voice.

Chapter 14

I stared at him blankly as I tried to come up with an answer. I took note of the dark circles under his eyes, the scruff on his chin, and the way his slightly greasy black hair fell into his eyes. His intense brown eyes cut right through me as he waited for a response.

He looked worn out and stressed, as were his clothes: an old faded green T-shirt and baggy blue jeans. A hard-working man trying to provide for his family, I felt empathy toward him.

My eyes reverted behind him to his wife holding Ethan, although he'd always be known to the world as Thomas. "I said, what are you doing here? Why are you standing outside our door?"

"Oh, I thought this was my sister's room number," I lied.

"Mhm," he said as his eyes focused on me like a hungry lion spotting a wounded gazelle. "You never answered my question though. Who are you?"

"I'm just here looking for my sister's room."

"You are still not answering my question. Who are you? You look very familiar."

My skin became hot and tingly. "I am—"

"Tom, what's going … oh." She stared at me with a shocked expression.

Here we go again. Just say it.

She regarded Thomas laying in a cradle by the bed. "You look just like our son." She laughed. I thought she was going to say something else. "Don't you think?" she asked Tom.

"He does."

I laughed along and said, "It was nice meeting you but we have to get going."

"Oh, okay. You two have a good night," the wife said, allowing us to turn around and leave. Ren and I were halfway down the hall when I looked over my shoulder behind me. Tom still stood in the same place with crossed arms and the same questioning look in his eyes.

"That was weird," Ren whispered to me. "He was about to turn us in."

"Either that or he was wondering why I look so similar to the son who looks nothing like him."

Chapter 15

Three days later in the early morning, I got myself ready to go out and find food. I must have been making too much noise because I woke Ren up.

"Where are you going?" she said groggily.

"To the city to find food. Do you want anything in particular?"

"No, I am fine with anything you bring. I'm just hungry." She laughed. I smiled, then sighed as I gave attention to the gnawing feeling of hunger that I'd been ignoring. I was thankful I had someone to go through this journey with. Something about her and her appearance made the expression on my face change, which made Ren notice too.

"Why are you looking at me like that?" she questioned.

I squinted my eyes as I asked, "Had we met before you volunteered at R.B.? I have been racking my brain for days because I feel like I have seen you somewhere before."

She tilted her head in confusion as she said, "No, I don't think we have ever met before. Why?"

I shook my head; I must have been imagining it. Until I had a revelation. The picture of the woman I had printed out about the dream she had of having a twin sister.

"No, I have seen you before. Look!" I pulled the folded article out of my pocket. I knelt beside Ren and pointed to the woman's picture.

"This woman looks just like you! I have been wondering why you looked so familiar."

Ren studied the photograph and a crease formed between her brows. "I look exactly like her. We even have the same freckles."

"She looks like your long-lost twin." I laughed, half serious.

Ren paused. "What if she is?"

"Ren, she's from the year 2040. I'm not saying she is your long-lost twin. I was just pointing out how much I think the two of you look alike." I didn't want to make her worry or over think.

"But what if she is?" She held the paper close to her eyes, almost touching her nose. "What if I am the twin who took decades to win her battle? Like Ethan?" I pondered this and realized it's not outside the realm of possibility. Anything was possible at this point.

"I want to know more about her."

"Then, I'll help you," I said with a smile.

"When all of *this* is over and we are not on the run anymore, I want to know anything I can about her life," she said, grinning at the paper. I had never seen Ren look this hopeful before and it felt refreshing.

"I can go to the market now and leave you to your thoughts if you would like. Or do you want to talk?"

"I'll be perfectly fine. You go ahead," she said, still radiating with hope.

——

I left Ren at the campsite and headed to the city to find the market. Her hopefulness rubbed off on me and I began to believe that today would be more *hopeful*. Other than at night, the early morning was the only part of the day where I could go out and gather supplies without having to worry too much about getting caught. On the walk there, I analyzed my life and the recent events I'd been a part of. Eventually, I went off on a tangent about how it hadn't been easy living in a van under a bridge. Especially with Ren as my company. Ren liked everything to be a particular way and it drove me insane. For example, she couldn't sleep unless all the doors in the van were locked. The windows, the sunroof, and the shade were all closed. She had to have her seat belt on, and I had to be lying beside her. I asked her why she did this every night, and she said it made her feel safe, which I found to be a very cute quirk.

In the span of a few days, Ren had become one of my closest friends. Someone who I could lean on for support, someone who I know will be there the next day when I wake up. I didn't want to admit it to myself amid all the chaos going on, but I did feel like maybe one day she could become more than my best friend. When I looked at her, I could tell that she felt the same way about me. For now, it is best that we leave it at that.

As I approached the broken city, my anxiety increased with the amount of people there. I assured myself it was just another riot. Through their yells and chants, I understood why they were so upset. Their society had fallen, lives had been lost, and people were confused. Yet, the more I listened to the yelling, I realized this was not a riot at all. They were listening to a speech, applauding the speaker. I threw my hood up, adjusted my sunglasses, and stood on the outskirts of the crowd. I was shocked at what I saw before my eyes.

That voice, I would know it anywhere. It was the same voice that would threaten me for information and scold me if I ever did anything wrong with the equipment. This was the same voice and man that forced me to become homeless: Paul Ezell.

I never should have said it would be a hopeful day.

Chapter 16

A wave of nausea washed over me when I looked at his face. I remembered the control he used to have over me and how scared I used to be of him. The dreaded cot he would have me lay in, the burning antidote that would run through my veins nearly every day, greeted me as a painful memory.

All the people in the crowd had a white pamphlet, with a title that read, "The truth about the pre-birth world." I nonchalantly read over a young boy's shoulder; the pamphlet explained the basic information of the pre-birth world. Paul took a deep breath.

"I am the founder of R.B. for those of you who do not know me. I am amazed at how many supporters R.B. has gained in these past few weeks. Even though our organization has now been turned to ash, R.B. still lives on through the people who are here today. With that said, I would like to announce that there is, in fact, a pre-birth world, and with the help of my assistant," he said, motioning to Michael who's beside him. "*I* was able to turn the theory of a pre-birth word into a tangible fact. One that I am eager to share with you all."

The crowd was completely silent as they waited for what came next. As he said this, he slightly raised a small brown leather notebook with his left hand that was coated in *my* fingerprints. This notebook belongs to me. It was the only thing in the universe that I could pour my heart and soul into and tell all my secrets to.

My grandfather gave it to me years ago and I had no idea what to use it for until I became a tester for R.B. After that, I began to log everything in the notebook, from the time that I woke up to the time that I went to bed. Everything was in there about my journey through the pre-birth world. I even sketched Ethan and the blue orbs.

"I am about to share with you what *I* found and what *I* witnessed when *I* was inside the pre-birth world." The crowd exchanged looks and quietly whispered among themselves while I felt my body ignite with anger. "I now know why most of us do not remember the pre-birth world. These horrors are something that we should shield our sons and daughters from. But as humans, we must know the origin of our existence. I—"

"How can we see ourselves?" someone from the crowd shouted.

"Your question will be answered very soon. First, you need to know how *I* successfully entered the pre-birth world."

Paul hesitated, flipping through the notebook to find the answer. Seeing him flip through the pages made me feel so vulnerable. He was reading my thoughts on paper, contaminating its pureness with his lies.

"When I entered the pre-birth world, I had no idea of what I might find. Although, what *I* did find seemed impossible to be true. Blue orbs, which I later discovered were new souls who had not yet seen a preview of their life, were floating around me," he said, recreating the sequence of events that happened.

"I heard a voice in my head, which at the time I thought nothing of. Off into the distance I saw a human figure.

Excitement exploded within me, thinking the figure was myself. As I approached the figure, I saw that it was a boy who looked almost identical to me, and I sighed in relief because the search was over. I found myself.

"The tables turned when I heard the voice again in my head, wanting desperately to grab my attention. The voice matched my own so perfectly, yet the urgency in his voice made me think otherwise. I asked who he was and what he wanted with me. I still get chills when I think about his response."

Furry swamped my body, blurring my vision. I wanted to say something but I knew it would be a terrible idea and it took everything I had to keep my mouth shut.

"Who was it?" someone from the crowd yelled.

"He told me that he was my unborn twin. That he had been trapped in the pre-birth world for twenty-two years, unable to get out." He paused and the crowd gasped softly. "So, to answer your question, sir, you have to collect the DNA from the soul and then mix it with your DNA. Without me, this entire project would have been impossible. You see, the only reason why I was able to see myself was because I am an identical twin. My DNA was already intertwined with that of my brother's soul. Once I am in the pre-birth world, I collect samples of other souls' blood as I watch my brother fight. This is how I will let you see your soul. Identical twins are the only way to share this world with the public."

"Sir, then why have I never seen a pair of twins in my lifetime?" a short woman in the middle of the crowd asked.

"I'm eighty-five years old and I have never seen a pair of twins either," a feeble old man to my left yelled. As Paul scanned the crowd with his eyes looking for the old man speaking, his eyes landed on me briefly. I lowered my head, willing myself to be invisible, although I would much rather prefer to slit his throat right there in front of everyone.

"This is because we were never supposed to have access to this world," he said with his eyes still locked on me. "How—"

Suddenly, his face became pale white as he clutched the notebook tightly. He opened his mouth, paying no attention to the question being asked, and said, "We are out of time, I will answer more of your questions later." Disappointed faces flooded the crowd as Paul sprinted off the stage and down the steps. The rage I had boiling inside me burst, searing everyone's skin around me. I bolted for the stairs and practically threw Paul back onto the stage. I took the notebook and threw it on the ground as the audience yelled in disapproval.

"What the hell are you doing?" I yelled in his face while pushing him back. "You know all of this is untrue!" Paul opened his mouth but someone from the crowd beat him to it.

"What the hell are *you* doing here if you aren't a supporter? Get out of here! No one cares about your opinion!" A woman from the crowd scolded me.

"That's right. What are *you* doing here?" Paul said in a condescending tone, this time pushing me back.

"You know why I'm here, Paul! You're not the one who experienced any of this! I am. You're the one who stopped me from finishing the experiment in the first place."

"I don't know what you are talking about, sir. Here, take a pamphlet to help clear up some of this confusion," he said calmly as he swiftly pulled one out of his jacket pocket.

"You know exactly what I am talking about! You know who I am!"

"Sir, I wouldn't recognize you even if I did know who you were. You are too covered up. Maybe if you could take off the sunglasses I would be able to recognize you," he said as he reached for the glasses, trying to blow my cover.

I pushed his hand away and said, "Stop. You're trying to change the subject. You know this isn't right!"

"Sir, just remove your sunglasses. I don't see why it would be a problem unless you have something to *hide.* Come on, if I knew who you were, maybe I could help you understand," he said with a repulsive smile. His eyes started to waver from side to side and he looked at something behind me.

Before I could finish my thought, someone pulled my sunglasses off and my hood down. The crowd gasped and whispered my name, staring up at me.

"I knew it was you!" The same short woman yelled as she grabbed my left ankle, digging her nails into my skin. I wiggled my foot free, accidentally kicking her chin in the process and causing her to shriek and stumble backward. Paul clutched my arm violently, but I escaped. I pushed past the man behind me and ran off the stage. Paul jumped on top of me, which made us both fall to the ground.

"No matter what you saw in there, it isn't your story to tell. R.B. is mine, the pre-birth world is mine, and as far as everyone knows, you had no part in it." Paul hissed. "No one will believe you anyway." He forcefully pinned my neck to the ground out of spite. I pushed myself to a standing position. Blinded by rage, I delivered a punch to Paul's chin. Even though my punch packed as much force as I could muster, the impact was not enough to seriously injure him. That is, until the two-foot-tall speaker, perfectly positioned behind him, caused him to trip and fall off stage. Paul landed on the crown of his head, breaking his skull.

His blood oozed from the gash in his head and he laid unresponsive. I looked up to the hundreds of people in the crowd; all had a horrifying look directed at me.

Murderer, was the only word that bounced in my head, and I now had a sea of witnesses to say what I am.

A murderer.

Chapter 17

As soon as the crowd realized the reality of the situation, they immediately rushed to Paul's aid.

"Paul? Paul?" a woman shrieked, laying her hands on his chest.

"Someone help! He's not breathing!"

Other bystanders rushed over and attempted to stop the bleeding that refused to clot. Paul remained unresponsive to the efforts and he slowly began to go limp.

The attention turned toward me and an uproar began as I felt their cold eyes lock in on mine. "It's your fault! You killed him!" Michael said as he tackled me to the ground.

"Someone, call the police!" a long-haired man shouted.

As I wrestled to free myself from Michael's grasp, other bystanders took the opportunity to restrain me until the police reached the scene.

"Paul was a brave and heroic man who sought to uncover the truth! Because of your selfish violence, we will never have peace!" a woman yelled from the depth of the crowd.

"He was lying! I'm the only person who has ever been to the pre-birth world! The story is mine!" I cried.

"Shut up!" the man beside me said as he kicked me hard in the abdomen. "The cops will be here any minute! Then you will pay for what you have done!"

In no time, the cops handcuffed my hands behind my back. Hundreds of people witnessed me forcing Paul off the stage that unfortunately ended in fatality. Even though it was an honest mistake and I never meant to kill him, my word would be overlooked by the hundreds who all claim I was a murderer.

As I was hauled into the back of a police car, I thought of Ren and how she remained at the campsite. I only hoped she had the sense to run and stay hidden. She has to know that she is on the wanted list and there is a grand prize pinned on her capture.

Second-degree murder. This was my charge for killing Paul. I was also charged with evading the police as I had escaped the police car to warn Ren of her imminent arrest. I had run about one mile in the direction of the bridge when I was inevitably tackled and restrained by the police once again. After what seemed to be a never-ending fight for control, I concluded Ren had probably already been found and arrested, given the circumstances. I justified that warning Ren would lead the police directly to her location and that I would not be helping her at all.

For the murder of Paul Ezell and evading the police, I was sentenced to twenty-five years in prison.

Epilogue

Life after my prison sentence seemed surreal. Our society had changed for the better as people gained access to the pre-birth world and there was no longer a divide between our society debating who was right and who was wrong. Paul's assistant, Michael, had carried out the mission of R.B. and successfully allowed the mixing of civilian DNA and that of the samples I had collected in the pre-birth world. With this, anyone who wanted to witness themselves in the pre-birth world could now do so. The beauty that had flourished from the pre-birth world expands far beyond the original message of R.B. Which was to remember where we come from. The new message of this world is to let themselves see firsthand that they have the strength to overcome any obstacles that life may throw their way. As the battle their soul fought was the first defining moment of their inner strength.

Shortly after my arrest, Michael also uncovered the truth about R.B. and admitted that Paul had stolen my research and accredited me for the work I had done for the company. He even extinguished the price on Ren's head, and later informed me that she was never arrested for the crimes she *never* committed. Michael also said that she moved north and had not been heard from in some time.

I felt relieved when I heard this. I never wanted her to get hurt by my actions as she was scarcely involved with R.B. Maybe someday we will cross paths again and reunite what could have been. But with the last twenty-five years being consumed with my imprisonment, I doubted she would remember me, let alone want to get involved with me. Besides, I have taken up a life of solitude, as Paul's death by my hands naturally deflects many people from speaking to me.

I now have two identities in our society. The man who ventured into the unknown and uncovered the pre-birth world, and the murderer. And I can assure you, I am not known by the latter.

My days are typically quiet and I scarcely find myself leaving my apartment for anything other than groceries from the market. However, on one slightly overcast, chilly day, as I walked down the city street to the market, I found myself wanting to converse with a stranger more than I had in years. I accidentally brushed against his shoulder, and I muttered "sorry," expecting the stranger to be taken aback when he recognized who I was. But he looked at me with his shiny green eyes and short brown hair and said with a grin, "No worries."

I stared at him and could not help but marvel at his appearance and the recognition of a bond I had not felt for twenty-five years. I locked my gaze on his eyes and extended my right hand to introduce myself. "Hi, I'm Jacob," I said as I tried to contain my smile.

"Hello, I'm Thomas. It's nice to finally meet you," he said with radiating positivity that I can't help but admire.

He knows who I am!

"You remember me?" I exclaimed as I felt tears pool in my eyes.

"Of course, I do! I studied your research at my university and I admire your work. One day, I hope I will be able to explore the pre-birth world and witness my first victory. I truly cannot believe I got the chance to meet you. My friends won't believe it." Of course, he doesn't remember me like I remember him. How could he?

"Would you mind talking with my friends and me? We would love the chance to interview you about your research!" he continued with such charisma.

After a subtle pause and a soft smile, I gratefully replied, "Okay."

I will finally get a chance to get to know him, my brother. The one I risked everything for. To the world, he may be only known by the name of Thomas, but he will always be Ethan to me. My twin brother, only twenty-two years apart.

He's a new soul, eager to explore and make a difference in this complex world. He will make mistakes and learn from them along the way, but that is the beauty of being alive.

Acknowledgments

I would not have been able to write this book without the incredible support from my family and friends. I began writing R Reality when I was fifteen years old, and my family and friends supported my dreams of being an author in the future.

I also wanted to give a special thank you to my fiancée and the support he gave me throughout the creation of R Reality. This incredible person instilled the confidence in me to finish writing R Reality and to never give up on my dream of being an author.

Mackenzie Truss was raised in a small town in North Carolina. She was born into a family of six, consisting of three sisters, one of which is her identical twin. She has been a life-long writer and now author of a young adult novella. As a child, she overcame a traumatic brain injury, which later inspired her love for helping children with disabilities. She graduated from the University of North Carolina at Charlotte in 2023 where she received a bachelor of arts in special education and a minor in psychology. While pursuing her college degree, she worked at a Direct Support Professional to care for adults with severe to profound disabilities. After graduation, she pursued her career as a high school special education teacher. She continues to advocate for individuals with disabilities to help them live their lives to the fullest.

Made in the USA
Middletown, DE
06 November 2023

42027910R00087